Daniel Pennac was born in Casablanca, Morocco. He has travelled widely, working at various times as a woodcutter, a Paris cab driver and an illustrator, before finally becoming a schoolteacher, a profession he remains passionate about. One of the most translated authors in France, his books for both adults and children appear in over thirty different languages. The Kamo stories in particular are extremely popular, with sales reaching one hundred thousand in France alone. Daniel's other books for Walker include *Dog*, the poignant and witty tale of a scruffy little pup searching for an owner to train and love; and *Eye of the Wolf*, an extraordinary, magical tale about an Alaskan wolf and an African boy. Daniel Pennac lives in Paris.

Books by the same author

Dog

Eye of the Wolf

KAMO'S ESCAPE

DANIEL PENNAC

translated by Sarah Adams

WALKER BOOKS

AND SUBSIDIARIES

LONDON · BOSTON · SYDNEY · AUCKLAND

First published 2004 by Walker Books Ltd
87 Vauxhall Walk, London SE11 5HJ

2 4 6 8 10 9 7 5 3

Original edition: *L'évasion de Kamo*
© 1992 Éditions Gallimard
Written by Daniel Pennac
English translation © 2004 Walker Books Ltd
Translated by Sarah Adams
Cover illustration © 2004 Marion Deuchars

This book has been typeset in Weiss

Printed in Great Britain by J.H. Haynes & Co. Ltd

British Library Cataloguing in Publication Data:
a catalogue record for this book
is available from the British Library

ISBN 0-7445-8353-5

www.walkerbooks.co.uk

Pour Sarah-Marie

A Bicycle Fit for a Hero

"There's no way I'm getting on *that!*" said Kamo. He was pulling a face and holding the bicycle away from his body, as if it had been dipped in treacle.

"Why not?"

Kamo looked at me quickly and hesitated before answering. "Because."

"Don't you know how to ride a bicycle?" I asked.

He smiled scornfully. "There are loads of things I don't know how to do. I couldn't speak a word of English last year, d'you remember? I managed to learn in three months. So riding a bike…"

"Exactly. You'll get the hang of it in a couple of hours."

"I don't want to get the hang of it."

"Why not?"

"That's my business."

I decided to be patient. I knew my friend Kamo well enough to realize that annoying him wouldn't get me anywhere.

"Kamo, Dad mended this bike specially for *you*."

He frowned. "Sorry."

"This bike is a piece of history, Kamo. It took part in the French Resistance. It even escaped a German ambush. Look."

I crouched down on one knee and showed him the two bullet marks. One bullet had gone through the frame (between my grandfather's calf and thigh, while he was pedalling faster than he'd ever done in his life); the other had made a hole in the rear mud-guard (by that time, Grandfather had got away).

My dad had decided not to patch up the damage. He thought Kamo would like the battle scars.

"I feel bad about your dad, but I'm not riding this bicycle," he said stubbornly.

"Would you rather have mine?" Maybe mine was easier for a beginner: spanking new, fast as lightning, zillions of gears. "You've got your eye on mine. Is that it?"

"I don't want yours or anyone else's; I'll never ride a bike and that's final."

"Have you sworn an oath or something? Look, millions of Chinese people get around by bike every day, so why not you? You just want to be different again, don't you?"

I was starting to get annoyed. Dad had spent hours making the bicycle good as new again, specially for Kamo. It was a wonderful Czech model from before the war, with lever brakes and chrome mudguards that looked like the bumpers on a Buick. It was a stunner.

I tried to explain as calmly as I could. "Kamo, when Dad and Mum and I come here to the Alps every spring, we go on bike rides, get it? We spend the whole day outside. And we have picnics. It's something we've always done as a family, ever since I was small, and I really like it."

But I must have sounded a bit angry, all the same, because he let go of the bicycle and turned to face me, wagging his finger.

"Listen, I'm not a kid and I'm not throwing a tantrum. I can't explain it, but I know something will happen if I ride a bike, so I'm not going to do it, and that's final. I don't want to cause any trouble. You three can go off on your trips like you always do, and I'll stay here and get supper ready." He smiled. "Don't worry. You know me – I never get bored."

So that's the way things worked out. At least for the first week. My parents and I (they'd got their tandem; I was on my bike) spent our days cycling up hills and down valleys and searching for springs under mossy boulders. We'd get home late in the evening, dead beat but happy, like city people when they rediscover the mountains. The house smelt of *pommes dauphinoises*; it smelt of sorrel soup; it smelt of chicken with crayfish: the house smelt of Kamo's cooking.

"That kid's a real chef," said Dad.

"I get it from my dad," answered Kamo. "He was a cook when he was young."

Sometimes the house also smelt of fresh plaster or paint.

"I had a go at the attic today," Kamo would say. "There was a leak in the roof."

"Was your dad a builder too?" asked Dad.

"My dad knew how to do everything," he replied.

Kamo's father had passed away a few years earlier. He died in hospital, after cracking one last joke.

"He even knew how to die…" murmured Kamo.

After supper we'd play cards or Scrabble (Dad

lost mostly, and Mum generally won), so Kamo and I wouldn't be alone again until the house was quiet and it was dark and we were in our bedroom. That was when the pillows started flying. Kamo was stronger, but I was quicker. What you've got to do in a pillow fight is duck and dive: get the other person's attention, pretend you're an easy target, duck – and then whack them back. Kamo's head vibrated like a punchbag. He went all weak at the knees, but just as I was about to finish him off, he uncoiled like a spring and caught me on the chin with his pillow, sending me flying across the room. Battering each other to death was our way of getting to sleep.

And we talked. You can't beat talking with the lights out. One evening, right at the beginning of the holiday, Kamo's voice came clear across the dark room.

"She shouldn't have done that to me."

Who was "she"? And what had "she" done to

him? He must have second-guessed my questions, because he continued.

"My mother shouldn't have gone off without me."

Of course! That was why he was spending his Easter holidays with us. His mother had gone away on a long trip. Starting off in Greece, then moving on to the Balkans and ending up in Russia. In search of her ancestors. "I need to find my roots," was how she'd put it to her son. And she'd entrusted Kamo to my parents for a few months.

"Her 'roots', as she calls them, are mine too, aren't they? She should have taken me with her."

Kamo's mother came from all over the place. From Greece on her grandmother's side, from Georgia on her grandfather's, from Germany on her father's (a Jewish hairdresser, who married the daughter of the Georgian and the Greek, and in the 1940s fled persecution by the "loony with the swastika moustache", as Kamo called him). A child of many horizons, Kamo's mother could speak umpteen languages, but she didn't really feel she was *from* anywhere. Or, as Kamo put it, she changed nationality like other people change their moods.

"No kidding – she goes to sleep in French and wakes up in Russian!"

The upshot of this was that when she felt a bit too German, or a bit too Jewish, or a bit too Greek, Kamo's mother would set off for one of her many countries of origin in search of her ancestors. If it was a short trip that coincided with the school holidays, she took Kamo with her. Otherwise she left him behind, which made him furious.

"You've got school, Kamo." And off she went for three months.

"Stuff school! Haven't the Balkans and Russia got plenty to teach me too?"

So that's where we were at: Dad, Mum and me on our wheels, and Kamo playing at being the chef back home.

But the business with the bike was still bothering me. In all the time I'd known him (we'd met at the childminder's), Kamo had never been frightened of anything. Could he really be scared of riding a bicycle?

"It's what's known as a phobia," Dad explained.

"A phobia?"

"That's right, a phobia. An irrational fear. Someone might be up for anything – walking naked into a cage full of lions, climbing Mount Everest on their hands, spending all night in conversation with the ghost of their tax inspector – but you show them the tiniest spider and they pass out. That's what a phobia is. And your friend Kamo has a phobia when it comes to bikes, that's all."

"Have you got any phobias, Dad?" I asked.

"Me? No, never had the slightest phobia. I'm a mega-dad!"

"Mega-liar, more like," interrupted Mum, laughing. "Don't you remember how scared Dad was of

Crastaing, your French teacher, when you were in Year 7?"

Towards the end of the first week I was woken in the middle of the night by the kind of thunder that drives dogs underground. The shutters on the bedroom windows lit up with each flash of lightning. The storm was right overhead. And Kamo's bed was empty.

At first I thought he must have gone to the kitchen to get something to drink, and I went back to sleep again. But when I woke a second time, Kamo wasn't back. I was worried, so I got up and put on my dressing gown and slippers. The storm was still bashing us about. Descending the wooden staircase, I felt like I was inside a huge crate with a maniac drummer beating furiously down on it.

No sign of Kamo in the kitchen. Or anywhere else in the house, which lit up and went dark again to the rhythm of the mad percussionist.

I opened the front door.

It was like stepping into a shower. I was soaked from head to toe instantly.

"Kamo! You idiot!" I roared.

I carried on blindly, fists clenched, convinced he'd ambushed me with a bucket of water. But it wasn't Kamo; it was the rain. Freezing cold rain falling thick and fast, flung in waves against the house by a wind fit to smash down walls. So there I was, dripping like a dishcloth, arms flying in the gale, when I saw him.

Kamo was crouched on the other side of the yard, under the wooden lean-to, so still that he looked like the old stump Dad used for splitting logs on. The lightning illuminated him against the night sky. And, just in front of him, the mudguards of the Czech bicycle shone with each explosion of light.

"Kamo!" I shouted.

He turned round. His face was streaming. It

almost looked like he was crying.

"Come inside – you'll catch your death," I ordered.

He followed me into the bathroom without a fuss, and we dried off before going back to bed. We were quiet now. Kamo was staring at the ceiling just like he'd been staring at the bicycle.

After a while I whispered, "You're really scared of it, hey?"

He didn't answer straight away. In fact, there was a long pause. And then he said, "No."

The storm was further off now, and the room was lit by moonlight. The house was silent.

"No. I'm really in awe of it; there's a difference."

More silence. And then he said, "Don't you think there's something sad about that bike?"

I didn't think so. I didn't see how a bicycle could be sad.

He went on. "It's as sad as a love that's been lost…"

By the time I decided to ask Kamo what he meant, it was too late: he'd fallen asleep. And all the storms in the world wouldn't have woken him.

Kamo and Mélissi

The miracle happened towards the end of the holidays.

Well, when I say "miracle" … let's just say it was a most unexpected event.

Dad, Mum and I were having a picnic in a valley, not far from the house. Kamo was going to join us later on foot, if he felt like it.

"It depends if I've got time — the attic needs painting."

"When you've finished the attic," Dad had said, and laughed, "you can start on the cellar: I spotted some cracks down there. And when you've fixed the house up, you'd better start on the world: it could do with some rebuilding!"

"My great-grandfather, the Georgian one, already tried to rebuild it once," Kamo had answered very seriously. "But things didn't work out too well."

As we munched our picnic, Dad said thoughtfully, "He's incredible, that boy; he really *does* know how to do everything!"

"It's ever since he's lived alone with his mother," explained Mum.

Lunch was nearly over and we were sitting on the fresh grass, singing Kamo's praises. Dad had opened the thermos and the smell of coffee was wafting over the valley, when Mum suddenly shouted, "Look!"

Our eyes followed her finger. A cyclist had turned off the road and was careering towards us across the field. He swerved between the rocks as cleanly as a downhill skier, and jumped the bumps like a cowboy on a bucking bronco. The mudguards flashed each time they caught the sun.

"Jeez," whispered Dad, "he's going to…"

But the bicycle always landed upright on the grass before zigzagging and flying up again. Each time it landed, the springs squeaked, the saddle groaned, the bell jangled and Kamo whooped, until, once he got close enough, he started shouting.

"She phoned! She phoned!"

The black bicycle was really a mad mustang with a shiny mane trying to send a cowboy flying as high as the moon.

"Watch out!" shouted Dad, leaping to his feet. "Brake!" And he began waving his hands like those guys in fluorescent caps on aircraft carriers when the plane looks like it might hit the water.

"*Stop!*" we all cried.

Mum and I were waving our arms in the air like Dad. But Kamo must have thought we were clapping, because instead of slowing down he let go of the handlebars at top speed and gave a victory salute to an imaginary crowd of fans.

The Czech bicycle flew up one last time. Instead of landing back on the ground, it plunged into a barbed-wire fence that we'd all seen, but which was hidden from Kamo's view by a clump of wild grasses. And Kamo carried on without his mount, arms spread out in space, like someone who'd finally discovered the secret of the birds. Only he didn't look much like a bird – more like a solidly built teenager who'd just crash-landed onto the remains of our picnic.

We shouted and rushed over. Three heads bent over him and six hands reached out to him, but all he did was open his eyes and say again, with a blissful smile, "She phoned."

His mother had called him from Georgia.

"I was up in the attic painting the skylight, when I realized it was time to get the food ready for tonight. So down I went to the kitchen to get the rabbit out of its pot, and what d'you think I saw stuck to the door? A message from the post office about a phone call. For me! I checked the time: one forty-five. And the address. I had ten minutes. There was no point walking there; I'd never make it in time. My first idea was to borrow your car. Pedals, gears, steering wheel – it couldn't be that difficult. But I had a quick look round and couldn't find the keys. That's when I thought of the bicycle. I literally jumped on it. I wasn't frightened any more! If my mum was phoning me from the other side of the world, I wasn't going to let some stupid bike get in the way.

"While I was pedalling to the post office, I remembered a story Big Louis told us last year. You know, the one about an uncle."

Big Louis, whose real name is actually Louis Lanthier, is a boy in our class who always seems to have loads of uncles or cousins, or friends of cousins, who've done amazing things.

"Anyway, it was the one about his uncle who is looking for incredibly rare butterflies in the

Amazon rainforest. Hey presto, the uncle gets bitten by a very poisonous snake. The sort that can knock you out in less than a minute. He rushes to his first-aid kit, gets out the antidote he always lugs around with him, and grabs the instructions. No joy – the instructions are written in Portuguese and the uncle doesn't speak a word of that language. But then a miracle happens, according to Big Louis: the uncle suddenly understands what's written in front of his burning, feverish eyes, as if he's just been given the gift of tongues. So he injects himself and saves his life. Big Louis claims his uncle now speaks Portuguese as fluently as if it was his mother tongue.

"We gave him a really hard time when he told us that story, remember? Well, we were wrong. At least that's what I told myself as I was heading towards the post office on this bike, because I felt like I'd been pedalling all my life!"

* * *

Kamo's mother had called him from Gori, in the province of Tiflis, Georgia, in the former USSR.

"Her grandfather was born in Gori," said Kamo.

"You mean your great-grandfather?" I asked.

"Yes, my great-grandfather. He was called Semion Archakovitch Ter Petrossian."

There was silence in our bedroom.

"But people called him something else," said Kamo.

It was that time of night when you confide in each other.

"They called him Kamo."

"Kamo? Like you?" I asked.

"Like me," he said.

"And your great-grandmother?"

"The Greek one? She was called Mélissi, and she was a singer. Kamo met her in Athens in 1912."

"Did you know her?"

"No, but I knew her daughter, my grandmother. She told me lots of things about the other Kamo, the original one. He fought against the Cossacks, and escaped from every prison they locked him up in. He was a sort of outlaw trying to make the world a better place, a bit like Robin Hood."

"How come they gave you his name?" I wondered.

"It was my great-grandmother Mélissi's wish. She wanted the first boy born in her family to be called Kamo, after *her* Kamo. They loved each other very much."

"And you were the first?"

"Yes. Mélissi gave birth to a little girl, my grandmother. My grandmother and her German husband had my mother, and my mother produced me. I was the first boy since the other Kamo in 1882."

"Does the name Kamo mean anything?"

"It means *flower* in Georgian. And d'you know what Mélissi means in Greek? That's what really gets me: it means *bee*."

Silence.

Then Kamo whispered with a smile, "Mélissi and Kamo ... a love story between a bee and a flower."

The Czech bicycle had valiantly survived the fall. Only Kamo's nose was a bit flattened. No more attic, no more cooking, from now on he'd go wherever we went. He wanted to be included on all our trips.

"What are we going to eat?" asked Dad. "Who's going to repaint the house, wax the floor, dig the vegetable garden, wash the dirty clothes and mend our socks?"

Mum laughed in the wind. "Put a sock in it and keep pedalling!"

What Kamo managed to do on that bicycle was breathtaking. He couldn't have looked more at ease if he'd been cycling all his life. That heavy, noisy old Czech rattletrap that looked like a pre-war car, with its enormous front light and gleaming mudguards, turned into a wildcat and was tamed. Each time he accelerated, he left my racing bike standing, in spite of its razor-thin profile. He would overtake me at full speed, stop dead in his tracks round the first bend, do a wheelie and cross in front of me while I was still trying to catch up with him. I couldn't work out how he did it – he must have had a jet engine stashed away somewhere under that heap of old metal.

"Kamo, let's swap!" I pleaded.

He was happy to lend me the bike, but as soon as I clambered on, it felt like the pedals had been stuck onto a machine that weighed at least fifteen tons.

"Don't wear yourself out," Kamo said. "I'm the only person it'll answer to."

"That kid's as strong as an ox," said Dad.

On one of our last evenings I asked him, "What about being frightened, Kamo?"

"Frightened?"

"You know, your bicycle phobia, the way you were 'really in awe of it'?"

He thought for a moment and then said, "It's like a dream, a dream I've forgotten about."

After a while he added, "You know, the thing about Big Louis is…"

"Yes?"

"Well, I don't think he's as stupid as he looks."

A little bit later he said, "We can do extraordinary things when we have to."

I giggled. "Like riding a bike, for example."

But Kamo wasn't laughing. "Yeah, like riding a bike when there's something inside you screaming not to do it…"

"D'you believe in premonitions, Kamo?"

Silence. Then Kamo replied, "If Caesar had listened to the oracles, his old friends wouldn't have stabbed him in the stomach." And then he added, "If King Henry II had listened to his wife, Catherine de' Medici, he wouldn't have come unstuck in that tournament."

"A lance in the eye."

"And out through his ear."

"Took him days to die."

"Can't have been very funny."

"No kidding…" I agreed. (When I think about it, those late-night discussions were really cool.)

"Anyway," said Kamo, "the premonition I had didn't come true."

We heard an owl hooting in the distance, and an engine purring as a car climbed the valley.

"When's your mother going to call you again?"

"Not for another month."

"How come so long?" I asked.

"She likes feeling free when she's travelling." There was no reproach in his voice now. Just the same admiration he always showed whenever he spoke about his mother.

"Kamo?"

"Yes?"

"What did you mean, the other day, when you said your great-grandfather, the other Kamo, tried to rebuild the world, but it didn't turn out too well?"

"The Russian Revolution," answered Kamo. "He was a revolutionary fighting for the cause."

A long silence followed. And then Kamo added, "That's what came between him and Mélissi the Bee."

"Why? Didn't she agree with his ideas?"

"No, it wasn't that."

The owl's hooting was getting closer. It always made its nest in our house at the end of the Easter holidays, just before we went away.

"It was something else," said Kamo. "I'm not sure there's room for two passions in a revolutionary's heart."

Much later, in the middle of the night, I heard him whisper, "He should have chosen Mélissi."

The Drama

Dad was at the root of the trouble, as the saying goes. Or rather, for a long time afterwards, my dad blamed himself for what happened. Not that I think he had anything to do with it. If I had to point the finger, I'd blame history. History with a capital H. The history we get taught at school, the history we find in books, the history that settles drop by drop, making our memories much older than ourselves. The history we create every day without realizing it. The history we know as life before it becomes history.

We were getting ready to set off. The car was loaded up. It was a family car with a boot so big you could have got a small elephant inside. All our bags and suitcases fitted in easily. But Dad had still fixed up the roof rack. I asked him why, and he hit his forehead as if he'd suddenly remembered.

"Jeez, you're quite right, I'd forgotten!"

Then he called out, "Kamo, the bikes, please!"

"The bikes?" asked Kamo.

"That's right, yours and your friend's."

This was Dad's way of giving the Czech bicycle to my friend Kamo. He was making a real sacrifice, because the bike had belonged to his father. It was a family relic, a heroic model that had taken part in the French Resistance. Kamo hardly knew how to thank Dad, but the look on his face spoke for him.

Later I found out that Mum hadn't liked the idea of taking the bikes back to Paris. "It's too dangerous," she had said.

But Dad had managed to convince her. "The little one's got his head screwed on, and Kamo always lands on his feet." It was the fun argument that had finally won Mum over. "It'd make them so happy…"

He was right. Nothing could have made us happier. Taking the bikes back with us meant being able to make the holidays last a bit longer. Maybe for ever.

"Can we go to school on them?" I asked hopefully.

"No, they're just for riding round and round inside the flat!" Dad said, and laughed.

Kamo and his Czech bicycle were a hit at school. Even the flashy kids with their compact Japanese frames were green with envy. All the in-crowd, who were up to speed on the latest models and the coolest gear, hovered around the historic bike with eyes popping out on stalks.

"What make is it?" someone asked.

"Pre-war Czech," answered Big Louis, who was really clued up about bikes.

"And what's that hole in the frame?"

"It's from a German ambush," Kamo said casually.

"Are there any bits left that'll still come off?"

"Try and see…"

As if the bike wasn't heavy enough, Kamo had fitted two enormous postman's saddlebags, made of leather and as old as the bike itself, which he crammed with stuff for class. When we got to school in the morning, we'd each take a bag and throw it casually over one shoulder, like cowboys hitting the saloon with our saddles on our backs. With a shrug, we'd offload the bags onto our desks, like saddles onto the bar, and Big Louis would call, "The usual? Two whiskies?"

Then came the cinema. The film started at midnight. Midnight was late, even for a Saturday. Even for parents like mine. But missing the film was out of the question. It was one of the first screen versions of *Wuthering Heights*.

"I'm not letting you out in Paris at midnight," declared Dad.

My father had made up his mind. But *Wuthering Heights* was Kamo's favourite novel. He'd read it in English at least a dozen times. He'd even translated it into French, because he didn't think any of the other translations were up to scratch. He'd fallen in love with Catherine, the heroine. He seemed to think he was Heathcliff and he was madly in love. We'd watched nearly every version that tried to make the novel work on the silver screen. Each time, Kamo came out of the cinema boiling with rage.

"What a turkey! That director didn't have a clue."

Each time, I found myself being yelled at as if I was the film director in question.

"And what about the actress playing Catherine?

I mean, *please*. And that idiot pretending to be Heathcliff. What a jerk wearing all that gel. People have no right to treat characters like that. Fictional characters should be treated with the same respect as real people. Don't you agree?"

I didn't have much choice.

So, each time our favourite cinema was showing an old version of *Wuthering Heights*, we rushed to see it. But this time Dad was like a rock. So Kamo tried to negotiate with Mum. He went to give her a hand in the kitchen, like he always did, and at suppertime that evening, when my nose was almost in my soup, I heard Mum saying very clearly: "Come on, darling…"

I looked at my mum; she was smiling the smile of great battles won. Dad could never resist her special cocktail of an autumn stare and a spring smile. And that evening was no exception. He just said, "I can't take them in the car; I promised Mr Plonk I'd mend his telly."

Mr Plonk, as he was known, was a former work colleague of Dad's who lived on the other side of the city, and who hated cheap wine, television programmes and being retired. Unfortunately they were the only things he had left in life. Being retired made him unhappy, so he'd knock back a bottle of plonk or two and settle down in front of the telly. The next day he'd ask Dad to come and mend it, because he'd reduced it to a scrap heap.

"It doesn't matter," said Mum. "They can take their bikes; they'll be sensible."

Yeah, right. At that time of night, with hardly anyone around, it's not easy to be sensible. Of course we promised, but with the first few turns of the pedals we were already racing in the Tour de France. I was bent double over my thoroughbred, shouting out to Kamo that I'd get him; I'd catch up with him one of these days.

"Never!" yelled Kamo. "No one'll ever catch me.

I can outstrip German bullets!"

If a policeman had been in our path that night, he'd barely have seen us flashing past. Which is a shame, because if we'd been stopped in time, the accident would never have happened.

What's really strange, when I think back on it, is that the first thing I remember is a huge peal of laughter. *My* laughter, ringing out in the streets of Paris.

I'd given up trying to catch Kamo. He was standing triumphantly on the Czech bicycle, arms spread wide, shouting at the top of his voice, "I'm coming, Catherine! Wait for me; don't die – it's me, Kamo. I'm on my way!"

I was behind him, cackling like a hyena.

"I'm coming to save you," shouted Kamo. "Trust me! I'm going to save you once and for all!"

I was giggling so much, my bike was zigzagging all over the place.

"I'm going to step inside that screen," Kamo was

shouting. "I'm going to rip you out of that film. You'll never have to play in one of those dud movies again, Catherine!"

The road dropped down steeply. Upright on his bicycle, with one foot on the saddle and the other on the handlebar, Kamo rode into the red glow of the city night as surely as a surfing champion riding the Pacific waves.

"I'm taking you to an island I know in the Caribbean, Catherine. No more films! No more Yorkshire mists! From now on it's crystal-clear lagoons and the gentle curves of coconut trees!"

From time to time someone appeared at a window, but we'd already flashed past. Kamo just carried on shouting.

"We'll drink coconut punch with the savage who's trying to follow me, because he's our friend!"

It was a black car. Travelling without lights. Very fast. On the wrong side of the road. Kamo wasn't exactly keeping to his side of the road either.

"I love you, Catherine! Wait for me, my love – I'm coming!"

The black car hit him in the bend of the road. The front light of the Czech bicycle exploded on impact. Kamo collided with the roof, but the car continued on its way, crushing the metal frame of the bike in a series of screeches and sparks.

"Kamo!" I yelled.

Kamo was flung into the air and, for a moment, I lost sight of him. Then he landed in the middle of the street, rolled onto the pavement, and crashed into the main entrance of a block of flats, where all the windows seemed to light up at once.

The other detail I remember gets mixed up with the flashing lights of the ambulance and police car. Kamo had fainted and they were moving him onto a stretcher, when I saw a trail of blood trickling out of his ear. I was shouting, but no one was taking any notice.

"The car didn't stop! It was on the wrong side

of the road and it didn't stop!"

And while I was shouting, I felt something go crunch under my foot. I bent down. Kamo's watch was broken. The hands were pointing to eleven.

White as Death

When his father died, Kamo was struck by how white the hospital was.

"I'll never paint the walls of my house white," he declared.

He could talk about white until he was blue in the face.

"It's not a colour, you know," he'd say. And: "The thing about white is, the cleaner it looks, the dirtier it is. A shadow on white is scum from the sky."

And: "White is death in hiding."

That's what I was thinking about as I paced up

and down the corridor in Accident and Emergency. They'd rushed my friend Kamo straight into the operating theatre. Dad was holding Mum's hand. They were both sitting on orange plastic chairs. Dad was so pale that his black moustache looked fake. Mum wasn't crying, which was worse. She looked like she'd never cry again in her life. And I was pacing up and down, past the green and orange walls. I kept saying to myself, He won't die; he won't die. People only die when the walls are white.

But hours later (the walls were still green and orange, but a pale purple dawn was already creeping over the rooftops), when I saw the surgeon come out of the operating wing and go up to Dad and Mum, when I saw his white shirt, white cap, white hair and white moustache, when I saw all that whiteness leaning over Dad and Mum – who bounced up so quickly that the surgeon took a step backwards – when I saw how exhausted he was, how pale and tired his lips were when he said the words "be brave ... very little hope ... double fracture of the cranium ... massive cerebrospinal haematoma ... he's a strong kid, but...", when I saw Dad's arm stiffen around Mum's crumpled body, I knew my friend Kamo was done for. The Czech bicycle had killed him. I had just lost my best friend. My only friend.

Nothing ever happens without us asking why. Events cry out. They need explaining. And someone to blame them on.

"In the Middle Ages," Kamo used to say, "when a disaster hit a village, they'd burn a witch, just like that. Events call for vengeance, you see. Blind justice. The German economy nosedives and the loony with the swastika moustache decides to kill all the Jews."

There was no stopping Kamo once he'd got going on the subject.

"Human beings don't need reasons, just scape-goats. Take our class. Whenever something goes wrong, we're not interested in why it happened: we blame Big Louis."

I remembered some of the ideas Kamo used to come up with in history lessons, making us laugh and think at the same time, and while I was re-membering I heard Dad, poor bloke, saying over and over again, "It's my fault; it's my fault! I should've listened to you, darling; I should've left the bicycles behind."

But Mum, who was sitting bolt upright and had hardly budged from her chair, said, "No, it's *my* fault; it was madness letting them out in the city in the middle of the night."

Alone in my bedroom, with Kamo's broken watch on my bedside table, I knew *I* was the one to blame. I should have taken Kamo's premonition seriously, instead of teasing him. I could see him now, the night of the storm, kneeling in front of the Czech bicycle, his face soaked with rain – although he must have been crying, in fact – and I could hear him saying, "No. I'm really in awe of it."

So you can imagine what the atmosphere was like at home: we were all looking for someone to blame, and panicking about being guilty. Except we each blamed ourselves, which made it even worse, because you can't defend yourself against yourself, or cheer yourself up.

"It's no good; it's all my fault," Dad would say.

"Oh, stop it; you know it's *my* fault," Mum would groan.

And when I was in bed, it was my turn. "It's *my* fault. I should have trusted his premonition."

Luckily life finds ways of fighting back against despair. Ways so unexpected, they amaze you.

I was stretched out on my bed – I hadn't even bothered getting under the covers – and my eyes were wide open, when all of a sudden I remembered something else Kamo had said during our holiday.

"You know, the thing about Big Louis is…"

"Yes?"

"Well, I don't think he's as stupid as he looks."

It was as if a firework had exploded, lighting up the darkness. I jumped out of bed and rushed to the phone.

It rang for a long time. The ticking of the hall clock marked the seconds. At last I heard Big Louis's voice, sounding faint.

"What kind of jerk wakes a family at four in the morning?"

"Me."

"Ah! You? What's up?"

"Big Louis…" To my amazement I couldn't say another word. If I told him about Kamo's accident, if I explained the state he was in, I felt I would kill him off for good.

In the end it was Big Louis who asked, "Has something happened to Kamo?"

And then I came straight out with it. Big Louis didn't interrupt me once. He was all ears. When I'd finished, he said, "Don't worry…"

I was waiting for the follow-up. For him to start coming out with the usual stupid remarks. "Come on, he's made of strong stuff; he's invincible, is our Kamo." That kind of thing. But not a bit of it. He said something quite different.

"Kamo isn't going to die." And then he added, "But it's up to us."

I gripped the receiver and waited.

"I've got a cousin," said Big Louis after a pause, "who split his head open falling from the sixth floor; he crashed through a glass roof and landed splat on the concrete garage floor."

I could feel anger welling up inside me.

"Have you noticed," Kamo once said, "how Big Louis always tells you about something extraordinary that happened to one of his cousins, or the friend of one of his cousins?"

"Well, we managed to save him," said Big Louis. "We saved him the same way we'll save Kamo. In *exactly* the same way."

"Meaning?" I was being sarcastic.

"By thinking about him," answered Big Louis, dead serious.

"Sorry?"

And, cool as a cucumber, he repeated, "By thinking about him. All we have to do is think about him night and day, and he'll pull through. We mustn't let him out of our thoughts. We must think about him every single second. If we can do it, if we never give up, if there are no gaps in our thinking, Kamo'll make it and the battle will be won."

He spoke as calmly as a doctor who knows they're prescribing the right medicine. I felt his confidence comforting me straight away. It was like being wrapped in a warm blanket of sleep.

"You're exhausted," said Big Louis on the other end of the line. "You're the one who's been thinking about Kamo until now, so go and get some sleep; I'll take over. I'll wake you when it's your turn to be on duty."

I fell asleep as soon as I'd hung up.

Kamo, Ka-mo,
Kah Moe, Car Mow…

Dad and Mum let me have a lie-in, and I got the day off school. The telephone woke me in the middle of the afternoon.

"Hi there." It was Big Louis. "Your turn to think about Kamo; I'm going home to get some shut-eye."

"How did it go today?"

"Great. Got two hours' detention in physics."

"What for?"

"Duh … maybe because I had something else on my mind?" He chuckled. "It'd have made Kamo laugh, that's for sure."

"Tell me about it."

"Oh, it was no big deal," said Big Louis, "just Plantard calling me up to the blackboard. I'm concentrating so hard on Kamo, I barely hear him say my name. So he calls me up a second time, and the class starts sniggering. Anyway, up I go to the blackboard. Plantard's firing questions at me. I'm keeping shtum.

"'Would I be right in thinking you haven't finished your homework, Lanthier?' Yes, sir, I nod, you would. 'And what's your excuse this time? Don't tell me you left your satchel behind with yet another of your cousins?' No, sir, I shake my head. No, sir. 'Well?'

"And that's when I tell him, 'I haven't finished my homework, sir, because I was thinking about something else, and I'm still thinking about it right now, sir, which is why I'm keeping shtum, sir.' The class explodes with laughter, but Plantard raises his hand. 'Would you like to tell us what you *are* thinking about, Lanthier?' 'Someone, sir.'

"That gets them going. 'Who're you thinking of, Big Louis? What's her name? Is she good-looking?' And Plantard – you know what he's like, always ready with a cheap joke – says, 'Come on, Lanthier, answer your classmates. Who were you thinking about so much you couldn't do your homework?'

"I decide to play it dumb. 'She's called Catherine, sir.' By this time, the class is yelling, 'Catherine! Catherine! How cute! Give us her phone number, Big Louis. Write it on the blackboard.' So I say, 'She's called Catherine Earnshaw, and she's the heroine of *Wuthering Heights*, the novel I was reading last night, sir.'"

Big Louis went quiet for a moment on the other end.

"Bingo. He gives me two hours' detention. But what's so funny is that it's all true. I read every word of *Wuthering Heights* last night, because it seemed the best way of thinking about Kamo."

Silence again.

"And I'll tell you something. It beats me why he's so in love with Catherine ... I mean, I think she's a pain in the neck. Definitely not worth chucking yourself at a car for." He was dead serious. And then he added, "But I guess that's Kamo's business. You know what he's like when he's in love; there's no talking sense to him."

Kamo was lying alarmingly still in the hospital bed. His face was wax and chalk. His eyelids were pale purple like the dawn sky the morning after his accident. For a moment I thought he'd stopped breathing. I leant over him. No. It was just that he was so still. And because he was wearing that bandage. That white bandage... But he was breathing. Very feebly. As if he was curled up at the bottom of his being, and it was the hardest thing in the world for his breath to escape, to get out, to reach "the great outdoors" as Kamo had called it one morning on holiday, taking in the Alps with a sweep of his hand. All you could see was the bandage, which sort of made things worse. If he'd been covered in bumps and scars, we'd have said, "That's Kamo for you – been in the wars again, typical! Not to worry, he'll soon get over it; he always does."

But for once Kamo's face was as smooth as a newborn baby's. Not even a scratch. Nothing. Just the white bandage cradling his head stiffly. I knew that my friend Kamo was broken inside. It's not like Kamo to be still, I kept telling myself as I stood by his bedside. It's just not like Kamo.

It suddenly hit me how childish we were being. How could thinking about Kamo stop him looking so pale and waxen, breathe life back into his stillness, heal him inside?

"It's one approach," said Dr Grappe, the school doctor, when I arrived panting at his surgery and told him about Big Louis's theory.

"D'you think it can work?"

Dr Grappe didn't give me a straight reply. But what he told me was better than a thousand answers.

"Real affection always inspires people to get better."

We *had* to think about Kamo. We had to think about him without ever giving up. Big Louis was right. And that's why I couldn't let Kamo's stillness give me the creeps. His stillness…

That's when I remembered the cat episode. It happened when we were in Year 1, at primary school. So we're not talking about yesterday. We were on our way home when a cat got run over in front of our eyes. Well, not exactly run over. It was a bit like Kamo's accident. The cat had tried to cross the road, but the wing of the car hit it in full flight. Even though Kamo nearly lost his balance when the cat shot against his chest, his arms closed instinctively around it. He just stood there, with the animal in his arms, watching the car go past. You could see the cat's tongue lolling out of its half-open mouth, a drop of blood forming on the tip. The cat had stopped moving. The kind of stillness that's different from sleep.

"He's dead," I said.

"No," said Kamo.

He walked calmly home with the cat in his arms, and climbed the two floors to his flat. When his mother opened the door, he went into his room without saying a word, slipped into bed without taking off his clothes (so as not to disturb the cat), and stayed tucked up, completely silent and still, for three days and three nights. On the morning of the fourth day, the cat finally opened one eye, then the other, yawned, and leapt out of Kamo's arms.

"See," Kamo told me, "when they're very ill, they pretend to be dead; it's their way of getting better. And if you keep them company, they get better more quickly."

*   *   *

At home, Dad and Mum were pacing around like caged animals.

"It's just unbelievable," Dad was saying. "We've simply got to find her!"

"I'll go to the embassy tomorrow," declared Mum.

"On the other hand," commented Dad, "the later she finds out…"

"I know," said Mum, "I know." She collapsed into a chair and cried soundlessly, repeating for the millionth time, "Oh my God, why didn't I listen to you?"

They'd spent the day trying to get hold of Kamo's mother. They'd gone to the travel agency responsible for organizing the trip. The travel agency had telephoned its office in St Petersburg – where the coach party was supposed to be. And it *was* still there, but Kamo's mother had disappeared.

"She must have left her group," I said. "She's gone on alone."

"Impossible," replied Dad. "You'd have to be mad to go it alone in Russia; it's chaos over there."

"But that's what she's doing," I insisted.

Dad suddenly stopped pacing up and down, and swivelled round to face me. "What do *you* know about it?"

"I just know."

And I did. On one of the last nights of the holiday, Kamo had chuckled and then said, "By this time, she'll be trying to give her group the slip."

"Give them the slip?"

"D'you think my mother went to Russia to take photos of the Kremlin with a bunch of tourists in shorts? She went in search of my great-grandfather, the other Kamo, the original one, and she'll find him!"

"Isn't he dead?"

"Of course he is; he was born in 1882 and died in 1922, at the age of forty. But Mélissi the Bee never wanted to tell us how he died. She knew all right,

65

but neither my grandmother nor my mother could ever get it out of her. It's a sort of secret, and now my mother's decided to find out the truth." Then he added proudly, "There's not a person alive who can make my mother follow the crowd."

For days now the hands of Kamo's broken watch on my bedside table had been pointing to eleven.

It's not easy thinking about someone non-stop. Even if that someone is called Kamo. And even if Kamo is your best friend. Your mind develops holes your thoughts can slip through. Your eyes stray to a photo of the mountains, your ear catches a note of music, and all of a sudden you stop concentrating on your maths homework, or thinking about your friend called Kamo.

At first I let the images of Kamo come to me, just like that. The most recent ones came first, of course: snapshots of the holidays, all jumbled up. Those late-night discussions, Kamo's recipes, the smell of chicken with crayfish, Kamo and the postman's saddlebags, the pillow fights, our bike rides in the Alps…

But then the tap dried up, until there were just a few drips left. So then I had to organize my memories, and start from the beginning. I remembered our first meeting at the childminder's (where we both fell in love with Mado-Maggie, who shook rattles under our noses), then nursery school, then the first years at primary school. I remembered Year 6 and Mr Margerelle, our teacher, getting us ready for secondary school by imitating all the teachers we'd have when we got there, and Kamo's enthusiasm for Margerelle the dreamy maths teacher as opposed to Margerelle the grumpy French teacher. I remembered Crastaing, a year later, the French teacher in Year 7, who scared everyone stiff except for Kamo. I remembered the amazing way Kamo had learnt English and got to know Catherine Earnshaw, the heroine of *Wuthering Heights*…

But when it was lesson time, or mealtime, or time to do my homework, the questions rained down, because everyone sensed I was somewhere else.

"Penny for your thoughts."

"How many times do we have to call you?"

"Would you mind concentrating for once?"

"Are you playing or not?"

It was torture trying to think under these conditions. When Big Louis rang me because it was his turn to take over, I'd hang up as exhausted as if I'd spent the day at the bottom of a mine, pushing a cast-iron cart loaded with Kamo, who got heavier and heavier.

And, of course, the inevitable happened. It was a Sunday afternoon, and I was in the bath. No one bothers you when you're in the bath. It's the perfect place for thinking. I was up to my ears in bubbles, desperately trying to find a new thought that might help Kamo. Poor Kamo. Even though I'd known him for ever, I felt as if I'd thought everything anyone could ever think about him. So I tried to picture his face: his shaggy plastering face in Dad's attic, the way his expression always went blank just before he told a joke, the face of Kamo in love with Catherine. I could picture all these faces, but then they started getting muddled up, until I couldn't remember a single one of Kamo's features. I'd been thinking about someone called Kamo non-stop for nearly a week, and I didn't have the foggiest idea what he looked like any more. My picture of Kamo had melted in my bath, along with the bubbles. At least I still had his name. Kamo's name, nothing else, just his name.

Kamo.

I started saying it over and over again in my head, because his life was at stake. *Kamo, Kamo, Kamo, Kamo, Kamo...* But there were two syllables in his name, and they soon got separated, as if I'd worn them out by repeating them: *Ka-mo, Ka-mo.* On their own they no longer meant anything – *Ka Mo* – and even their spelling began to slip away: *Kah Moe, Car Mow...*

The bath had gone cold when I woke up. *So* cold.

When Big Louis finally picked up the phone and said hello in a very sleepy voice, I yelled, "Big Louis! I stopped thinking about Kamo!"

There was a deathly silence at the other end of the line.

"I went to sleep in the bath."

Big Louis hung up without a word. I rushed to the hospital.

Djavaïr

Big Louis had got there before me. He was standing beside Kamo's bed, his lips trembling, his eyelids puffy, and he looked at me. Kamo's lips were blue with cold. So were the tips of his fingers. I touched his hand, but let go of it again with a start. It was as cold as my bath. Exactly the same temperature.

"It's over," said Big Louis.

Kamo was completely frozen now, like an iceberg slowly drifting away from us, out of reach.

"We'd better ring for the nurse," said Big Louis.

But neither of us moved. Our eyes were glued to Kamo's face, although it was very hard to recognize him. All you could see was the white bandage like a terrifying ice mask. Big Louis's hands hung down by his sides, huge and helpless.

"We'd better ring," he said again. He looked for the bell, his eyes blurry with tears.

We had to ring. We had to ring for someone to come and take Kamo away. For the last time.

Big Louis finally spotted a square button with a picture of a nurse in a white uniform. He looked at the button as if the whole hospital would blow up when he pressed it. Then he looked at me, and I nodded. His finger moved towards the bell.

"Don't touch that, you idiot!"

Big Louis couldn't have jumped higher if the bell had electrocuted him.

"What did you say?" he asked me.

I hadn't said anything. I was looking at the door, which Big Louis was facing. There was no one there.

And we were the only ones in the room. Apart from Kamo. But Kamo hadn't moved. He had the same bluish face imprisoned inside the ice mask, the same hands on either side of his gaunt body, skinny as a sparrow's claws. So we stared at the bell again.

"I'm *so* cold!"

It wasn't the bell that had just spoken.

Big Louis was the first to realize what was going on. He fell to his knees by the bed, and with his mouth pressed close to Kamo's ear he asked, "Are you cold?"

A few seconds went by and Kamo gave no sign of responding. Then we saw his blue lips clearly say the words: "Djavaïr, I'm too cold. Find me a pelisse…"

Kamo had spoken! Kamo had spoken, and it felt as if *we* were the ones being resuscitated! I rushed to the radiators: they were boiling hot. I closed the window and opened the cupboard doors: no sign of a blanket. Big Louis was still watching Kamo's lips, and he signalled at me to stop making such a racket. I froze on the spot, and clearly heard Kamo say, "I need a pelisse, Djavaïr, or I'll never get out of this hole!"

I wondered who Djavaïr was, but Big Louis was wondering something else. "What's a pelisse?"

"A fur-lined coat," I said.

There was a glint in Big Louis's eyes. He took off his jacket and spread it over Kamo's chest, whispering, "There you go, old man – it's the warmest pelisse in the world."

But it wasn't a warm coat. It was one of those cotton work jackets Big Louis's dad made his eight children wear as soon as spring was in the air. (In winter they wore thick corduroy trousers and workmen's jackets.) It wasn't warm at all. But when I went to find a proper blanket, Big Louis raised his hand.

"Leave it!" he demanded.

And, sure enough, over the next half-hour,

Kamo's colour began to return. His body was warming up in front of our eyes.

"Unbelievable," whispered Big Louis. "It's like watching mercury rise in a thermometer!"

Kamo's fingers could bend again, and his face was Kamo's face once more. He smiled faintly and whispered, with his eyes still closed, "Now, anything's possible."

Just then the nurse (the one we hadn't rung for) came into the room.

"What's this jacket doing?" she asked straight away. "Don't you think it's warm enough in here?"

She was a big woman from Martinique with a loud voice and quick gestures. She half opened the window I'd just closed, turned the radiators down and glanced at the temperature chart, while Big Louis, to my amazement, picked up his jacket and put it on as if nothing had happened.

The nurse leant over Kamo and said with a big smile, "You look a bit better today, sweetheart.

That's right, keep up the fight. I know you're going to make it." Then she turned to the two of us. "You've got to talk to him, boys; you've got to pretend he can hear you. But don't bother covering him up too much."

And out she went, as fast as she'd come in. I got up to close the window and turn up the radiators.

"Don't bother," said Big Louis. "She's right."

Then, taking off his jacket again, he said, "It's too hot in this room anyway. The cold he's feeling is inside him."

He threw back the sheets and blankets, covered Kamo's chest with his work jacket and made the bed again, taking care to keep the jacket well hidden.

Big Louis and I walked along in silence. We didn't take the metro. We walked through the city as if it was empty, as if it belonged to us. It felt like it was just us and the trees. And we were so happy, we could have made them blossom. Who says there aren't any trees in Paris? Trees are all you can see when you're happy.

But after quarter of an hour, I couldn't help asking, "Who d'you think Djavaïr is?"

"I don't give a toss."

I was taken aback, but Big Louis laughed that slow, special laugh of his.

"Everyone knows what an idiot I am," he said after a while. His hands were pushed right down in his pockets and he was walking with his head to one side, as if mesmerized by his own gigantic feet. "I've given up trying to understand; I just follow orders," he said. But he was smiling.

"My friend asks me for a pelisse? I find him a pelisse. My friend calls me Djavaïr? Why not? As long as he comes back to life."

The travel agency had turned Russia upside down and inside out, but there was no trace of Kamo's mother.

"I mean, for goodness' sake," stormed Dad, "someone can't just disappear like that!"

"On the other hand," said Mum, and not for the first time, "the longer it is till she finds out about Kamo, the better..."

My parents visited the hospital every day too. They stood by Kamo's bedside for ages and then came back home, Dad's arm round Mum's shoulders. The evenings always dragged out in the same silence. From time to time, one of my parents would shake their head, as if to say, "It's all my fault..."

I wish I could have cheered them up that evening, but Big Louis had said, "No way! Don't tell them Kamo talked!"

"Why not?"

"I don't know."

He was wild, and I could see the panic in his eyes.

"I don't know ... I just think ... nobody else should know about this – promise me." He'd turned round and was staring fiercely at me. His enormous hands were clenched in his pockets.

"Promise!"

"All right, Big Louis, all right. I won't say anything, I promise."

All the same, that evening, when I saw how
unhappy Dad was, and when I saw how unhappy
Mum was, I couldn't stop myself saying, "Hey, you
two..."

Dad lifted his head very slowly. I only called them
"you two" when we had something to celebrate.

"Kamo's going to make it," I said.

Dad stared through me as if he hadn't heard. I
burst out laughing and said, "We teenagers have a
sixth sense that you old fogies don't have any more."

Neither of them smiled. So I sat down next to
Mum and put my arms around her. "Mum, do you
trust me?" I asked.

She nodded. The tiniest yes.

"Well then, listen to me: Kamo's going to make
it." And I added, "I promise you."

Kamo and Kamo

Big Louis was right: Kamo's condition had to be kept a secret.

Kamo had his own way of making us understand this. As soon as anyone else came into the room, he stopped talking. And he didn't just go quiet – his face turned alarmingly pale and slightly blue again. Big Louis would become expressionless too and, even if he'd been laughing a second earlier, he'd suddenly look in the depths of despair. In fact, he'd look so glum that one afternoon the Martiniquan nurse lost her temper.

"If you carry on being miserable, I'm throwing you out of here! Your friend doesn't need weeping old women; he needs strong friends who've got faith in him getting better."

Behind his closed eyelids, Kamo was definitely talking. It was hard to tell if he was talking to us, or even if he recognized us, but he knew someone was there, right beside him: someone he trusted completely; someone he could say anything to and ask anything of.

He still called us Djavaïr, but he called us by other names too: Vano, Annette, Koté, Braguine... He asked favours from us, he gave us orders, and we obeyed, as if we really were Djavaïr, Vano, Annette, Koté, Braguine... Sometimes he would stifle a shout or roar with anger.

"Stolypin," he growled between clenched teeth, "you'll pay for this!"

Or: "Jitormirski was the one who betrayed me, that

villain Jitormirski! He was working for the Okhrana."

Or else he suddenly boasted, "I'm not afraid of the *gardavoïs*! They're small fry…"

And: "I'm too tough for the *nagaïka*!"

But whenever someone came into the room, he turned into the pale, speechless Kamo whose face gave no grounds for hope. The moment the intruder left, a smile would appear on his lips.

He always said the same thing. *"Yarost!"* Always the same word, hissed between closed lips, as if it came from deep inside him. *"Yarost!"* And all behind eyelids that never opened.

It didn't make sense.

And it went on for over a week.

A week of rambling remarks from Kamo, who was completely still, apart from slightly moving those thin lips of his.

To begin with I was really frightened. "He's raving mad," I said.

"So what?" Big Louis answered. Big Louis never

seemed to get worked up in these situations. "Would you prefer it if he was stone dead?"

"No, of course not."

"At least it shows there's something going on inside his head."

"Of course…" I trailed off.

"Anyway, he might not be mad. Maybe he's just dreaming, simple as that."

"Yeah…"

"Don't worry. He's pulling himself together, is our Kamo, I can tell. We just have to make sure we don't let him go, that's all," said Big Louis firmly.

I decided to do some research.

"Dad, what language d'you think *yarost* comes from?"

"Search me," he answered, without even bothering to look up.

I tried Miss Nahoum, our English teacher. "Can you tell me which language the word *yarost* comes from, miss?"

"I don't know, but you could try asking Miss Rostov."

Miss Rostov was the Russian teacher. She came into school once a week, on Thursdays. She was round as a Russian doll, and spoke with a reedy voice.

"*Yarost?* It means *fury*. In ancient times there was a very powerful god called Yarilo, the god of creative energy."

The name Stolypin, which put Kamo in such a rage, didn't mean anything to anyone. Until I asked Mr Baynac, our history teacher.

"Stolypin? Yes, of course I know who he was: the Russian minister for the interior, before the Revolution – the chief of police, if you like – and he was prime minister as well. He died in 1911, when he was assassinated in a theatre. Why d'you ask?"

He knew everything. He answered all my questions, just like that.

"And the Okhrana, sir?"

"The tsar's secret police. Are you interested in the Russian Revolution?"

I nearly spilt the beans, but I remembered just in time that Kamo wanted things kept secret. So I made something up.

"It's for a friend, sir, who's reading a Russian book from that period. There are loads of words he doesn't understand."

So he taught me that *nagaïka* was a terrible whip used by the Cossacks, and that *gardavoïs* were the equivalent of policemen in tsarist Russia. Thanks to Mr Baynac and Miss Rostov, all the icy words that Kamo had come up with in his hospital room began to mean something. Kamo was talking about his great-grandfather, the revolutionary. But I never asked the adults who Djavaïr, Vano, Annette, Koté, Braguine were... I reckoned they were part of Kamo's secret, and that naming them, just naming them, would be an act of betrayal.

*   *   *

In the half-light of his hospital room, Kamo whispered, "Onions, that's what I need. Djavaïr, *please*, get hold of some onions for me to stop the scurvy."

A few hours later, Big Louis slipped two onions under Kamo's sheets. He put them in his hands, closing each finger around them and watching his face all the while. A smile passed across Kamo's face as briefly as a shadow, or the flap of a wing.

"And sugar too. Djavaïr, I need sugar to get my strength back."

Big Louis brought him some sugar.

The next day the sugar and the onions had disappeared.

Kamo's lips were twitching very fast.

"The first time the Cossacks caught me was in Tiflis. I was wounded with five bullets in me, but I was still standing. They threatened to cut off my nose; they made me dig my own grave; they put a rope around my neck and the rope broke. I hopped around, playing the innocent, pretending to be an idiot. I sang while I dug my own grave, I played with the rope and I laughed. So they transferred me to the fort at Méteckh. They kept asking the same question: 'Do you know Kamo?' That's right, they weren't convinced it was me. I always gave the same answer: 'Of course I know kamo.' And I would take them to a ditch and show them some flowers. Back home, in Georgia, the word for flower is *kamo*."

Kamo's lips seemed to be running now.

"I didn't stay long at Méteckh, or at the prison at Batoum, or at the terrible Mikhaïlovski hospital where they locked me up with all the madmen, or in the Turkish prisons. There wasn't a place I didn't escape from. I won't stay long in Siberia either."

A long silence followed, and then: "*Yarost!*"

And, very quietly, in a whisper, behind those tightly shut eyelids: "The onions and sugar have given me strength again, Djavaïr. I'm ready. Bring me a strong file. Hide it in a loaf of bread. I need it tonight."

Big Louis didn't ask any questions. He just did what he was told. But I was frightened. This wasn't my Kamo, this person with shut eyes who whispered furiously in his hospital bed. It was the other Kamo, the revolutionary, the great-grandfather, the one who'd tried to change the world; the Kamo who'd abandoned Mélissi for the Revolution. He wasn't the one I wanted to bring back to life. I wanted my Kamo, the one who called out Catherine Earnshaw's name while pedalling like crazy in the middle of the night. I wanted my friend.

But Big Louis was following orders. And, well, I followed them too. That evening, I asked Mum to teach me how to make dough.

"D'you want to become a baker?"

"No, Mum, it's for a birthday at school: everyone has got to bring along something they've made themselves."

Mum was too tired to talk about it. She just taught me. As soon as she and Dad had gone to sleep, I let

Big Louis into our flat. He'd pinched two files from his dad's workshop.

"Files get broken easily. You have to think of everything when you're planning an escape."

I made two loaves of bread. We pushed the files into the dough and put the loaves in the oven. The first loaf split open while it was baking. There wasn't enough dough around the file. We had to do it again. The clock was ticking. Big Louis was getting nervous.

"He said tonight."

"I'm doing my best; I'm not a baker," I protested.

Apart from this brief exchange, we didn't talk. We just let the smell of warm bread waft over us. I told myself I was crazy, letting Big Louis drag me into Kamo's madness. But I could see that Kamo was getting better since he'd started talking to us. He'd got stronger. He was more like his old self.

I didn't go with Big Louis to the hospital that night. He'd slid a pencil under the latch of Kamo's window. The room was on the ground floor. He was going to push the blind up and get in, no problem. Then he'd put the two loaves of bread in Kamo's hands. He didn't need me for that.

"You're too scared; you'd give us away," he said.

He was right. I was scared. But I didn't know why.

Would Kamo's bed be empty tomorrow? And if so, which of the two Kamos would have escaped: mine or the other one?

I couldn't get to sleep that night. As soon as I closed my eyes, I saw a furious Kamo jumping out of the hospital window and heading off into Paris. He didn't look like my Kamo.

The Siberian Wolf

No. The next morning he was still in his bed, as motionless as ever, and still with that white mask around his head. Nothing had changed.

But Big Louis whispered in my ear, "He did it. He escaped."

I looked at Kamo's thin face more closely and, sure enough, yes, there *was* something of the old Kamo about it. He looked more relaxed. It reminded me of the way his face had lit up on holiday, when we were staring at the Alps. It was the face of Kamo free, back in the great outdoors.

Big Louis slid his hand carefully under the sheets. He pulled out two files. One of them was broken.

"You see? You can't be too careful. Leg-irons and prison bars are made to be strong."

That frightened feeling, which had left me for a moment, washed over me again in a great wave when I saw the broken file. I heard myself stammer, "And what about the bread?"

"Not a crumb left," said Big Louis. "He ate the whole lot."

I must have turned whiter than Kamo's bandage, because Big Louis added, "You should get something to eat too, you know. You look like you're about to faint."

Kamo didn't say a word that day. Or the days that followed.

"Why isn't he talking any more?"

Big Louis shook his head slowly, as if I didn't have the first clue. "D'you know what Siberia's like? It's a desert full of snow. Who are you going to talk to in a snow desert? He's escaped, and now he's got to cross Siberia."

We got really carried away this time. We sat on either side of the hospital bed, convinced the poor body lying there was battling it out alone, against the great desert of Siberia.

Every night, I had nightmares. The image of the broken file kept haunting me. I would wake up with a start and sit bolt upright, only to remember it wasn't a dream after all, we'd *really* found the broken blade, and it was just as if Kamo had *really* escaped. Going back to sleep was out of the question. On my bedside table the hands of the broken watch were pointing to eleven.

Kamo stayed quiet for days. And though it took us a while to realize it, he was getting weaker. His face was all puckered up; he was losing his body heat. Big Louis tried putting his jacket under the sheets again; it didn't do any good. It seemed as if nothing could ever warm Kamo up again. Big Louis was getting thinner every time I looked at him. And as for me, I felt like I'd never be able to shut my eyes again.

Then, one day, Kamo spoke.

"Siberia is one big belly of ice…"

Big Louis answered my stunned look with a sly smile, as much as to say, "Told you so. He's in Siberia."

Kamo went on talking. "Siberia swallows things raw, consumes them whole, and gives nothing back."

He spoke so quietly we almost had to put our ears to his lips. The breath coming out of them was frozen.

"But no one eats Kamo…" He gave a sort of frozen chuckle. "And you won't eat me either, Wolf."

Wolf? What wolf?

Kamo didn't say any more that day.

*   *   *

Back at home, Dad and Mum were starting to worry about my health. They'd been so preoccupied with Kamo up until now, they'd almost forgotten I existed. By the time they realized what was going on, I'd lost nearly six kilos and I'd slept so little that my eyes were glowing like coals in their red sockets. Action stations! A double helping of soup and lamb chops. They called Dr Grappe, who came round to give me an injection.

"Doctor, has any prisoner ever been able to escape from Siberia?"

He pulled the sheet up over my sore bottom and said, "There's no prison a man can't escape from."

Even with a starving wolf on his heels? But I didn't say that; I kept it to myself.

Kamo had been talking about the wolf again. It was a big old grey he-wolf with yellow eyes, who'd been following him for days. He was as exhausted as Kamo, and just as hungry too. At night, when Kamo couldn't find any wood to make a fire, they sat face to face, staring into each other's eyes. The wolf was too famished to be sure of his own strength. He was waiting for the man to fall asleep.

"What frightens me most about you, Wolf, isn't your teeth, or the way you stare at me, or how long you're prepared to wait..." Kamo was talking to the wolf. "What frightens me most about you, is the fact that you're all skin and bones."

The wolf terrified him, but he also kept him company.

"I'm skin and bones too; you're right to be wary of me, Wolf. You should always be scared of a man who's skin and bones."

Sometimes Kamo lit a fire. Then he and the wolf would go to sleep. The question was, who would wake up first and attack while the other was still sleeping?

"You're not the only one who's hungry," growled Kamo. "I've got teeth too, you know."

But one morning the wolf's teeth really did wake him, gnawing at his ankle. The wolf was tugging jerkily. Kamo had been wise enough to go to sleep gripping the largest branch from the fire, and the firebrand made an arc in the air as it swooped down onto the beast's muzzle. Then came the cracking sound of wood and bone. The wolf leapt backwards and the air was filled with the stench of grilled flesh and fur, but he didn't cry out.

"Bad luck, Wolf! You can eat my feet, but you aren't going to stop me making it to the railway line that goes to Vladivostok. Nor is Siberia. We're only three days away from the train now, so hurry up if you want to eat me."

Big Louis wasn't interested in knowing exactly where Vladivostok was.

"Things can go one of two ways: either Kamo makes it to the railway line, and he's saved, or he doesn't, in which case he's done for. Either way, I don't care where Vladivostok is."

But *I* needed to know. I felt it would bring me closer to Kamo. It was as if I was getting ready to wait for him, out there, on the station platform. That evening I looked up Vladivostok in the atlas: it was the most far-flung town in the Russian empire, and it was the last stop on the Trans-Siberian Express. That vast railway line divided the map in half in a clean sweep. Kamo was three days away from the line…

And then his mother announced that she was on her way back. The phone rang, and it was her. Yes, she'd left her group; no, she hadn't disappeared; yes, she'd come to an arrangement with the local authorities…

Dad was asking questions at random, but he didn't say a word about Kamo. He was making desperate signs to Mum, but Mum was shaking her head: she couldn't help him.

"No, he isn't here," said Dad all of a sudden, "not at the moment, no…"

He listened and just nodded his head, as if Kamo's mother was in front of him. Yes, yes, he kept nodding, but his eyes were blank. He was thinking of something else.

"Yes, Tatiana, you can count on me. I'll tell him." And he hung up.

"She's coming back at the end of the week," he said. "She's travelling on the Trans-Siberian Express. "She says it's snowing. What a country … it's spring here, and it's snowing out there!"

Then he added, "I couldn't bring myself to tell her about Kamo. I simply couldn't do it."

Kamo was in a very bad way. Sure enough, it had started snowing all over eastern Russia. The snow was falling so thick and fast that Kamo and the wolf couldn't see each other any more. Kamo could smell the wild beast on his heels; the animal could smell the bitter scent of man, just a leap away. But the wolf didn't have the strength left to leap, any more than the man did to escape. They sank deeper into the snow at every step. It was as if Siberia was sucking away whatever strength they had left.

"I hadn't counted on it snowing," murmured Kamo. His lips were pale and thin. "All this white falling everywhere…"

I suddenly remembered what white meant to him.

"D'you understand, Wolf? The snow's going to eat us; the sky's swallowing us up."

We could hardly hear him any more. The tiny wisp of air that escaped his lips seemed to trace the words in the air in invisible ink. And as soon as he'd spoken they evaporated in the stifling heat of the room.

I bent over and whispered urgently into Kamo's ear. "Kamo, your mother's on the Trans-Siberian Express, somewhere along the line, very near to where you are. She's there, Kamo!"

But he didn't answer. He'd stopped talking.

* * *

We were wandering about in Paris, in no hurry to go home. We were alone.

"Well, he'll have put up a good fight," Big Louis said again. "Have you noticed how there's no blossom on the trees yet? Spring's late this year."

And I replied, "There aren't any trees anyway, in this stupid city."

In my bedroom, on my bedside table, the hands on Kamo's watch still pointed to eleven.

The Hands
Pointed to Eleven

I wasn't surprised to find Kamo's bed empty the next day.

I'd spent all night picturing it. I hadn't said anything to Dad and Mum, but when I stared hard at my bedroom ceiling I could see Kamo's bed very clearly. Empty.

Big Louis and I didn't want to stay in the hospital a moment longer.

"Let's get out of here."

We hurried down a series of corridors, towards the main exit. The pale blue linoleum glinted like ice under our feet, even though the air was warm and still and stuffy with hospital smells: bad cooking and disinfectant. Big Louis walked so fast, I had a hard time keeping up with him.

When he disappeared round a corner, I heard metal clanging, someone swearing, the muffled sound of a fall, and a very angry voice shrieking, "Can't you look where you're going?"

I ran and found myself in front of the big Martiniquan nurse who'd been looking after Kamo. She was pushing a long stretcher on wheels and Big Louis was writhing about in agony on the floor, both hands gripping his lower leg. The body lying on the stretcher leant to one side, and a familiar voice rang out. It seemed to fill the hospital.

"Broken your leg, Big Louis? D'you want to share a room with me?"

Kamo. It was Kamo! He'd woken up. Pink as a baby's bottom, and chuckling just like Kamo. Kamo! Then he saw me.

"Hi there!"

The nurse held out a hand to Big Louis, who winced as he tried to stand up.

Kamo! Kamo's voice.

"Just got back from radiology. They tell me my head's healed quickly with a capital Q, but the last few days were touch and go." He tapped his head, which was shaved all over. "I look like a criminal, don't I? People are going to think I've just got out of the nick."

He was laughing.

Kamo didn't remember a thing. He couldn't even remember that he'd been dreaming. He really enjoyed our story about the prisoner, the escape and Siberia. But he was still weak. And he spoke very faintly.

"I must have rehashed the stories my grand-mother used to tell me when I was little, to send me to sleep at night: the adventures of the other

Kamo, her father, the Russian Robin Hood. I used to look forward to them every evening. Kamo was quite a character, and he really did escape from every prison they tried to lock him up in. But there's one thing that puzzles me: he was never deported to Siberia. The last prison they sent him to was the penal colony at Kharkov, in the Ukraine. The Revolution got him out of there, in 1917."

"But the file, Kamo, what about the broken file?" asked Big Louis.

Kamo laughed. It was the happy, tired laugh of a convalescent.

"Files aren't made to go in the oven, Big Louis. It must have been faulty, which is why it broke while it was being baked."

"And what about the wolf? And Siberia?"

I was asking the questions now. Kamo thought long and hard.

"I reckon I must have mixed up lots of different things," he said at last. "First of all, Dostoevsky's

Memoirs from the House of the Dead, which is set in Siberia – mind-blowing! And a short story by Jack London called 'Love of Life', about a man who's lost and alone in Alaska, and tries to reach the sea on foot, through the snow, followed by an old wolf who's in as bad shape as he is. It's a great story, and it made a big impression on me."

Kamo had to keep taking short rests when he'd been talking a lot. But we could see his strength coming back to him: it was like seeing a balloon being blown up.

"Memory's a funny thing, isn't it?" he whispered. "Like a cocktail shaker: you jiggle it about and everything gets mixed up."

"Who's Djavaïr?" asked Big Louis.

"She was my great-grandfather's sister, and she helped him escape several times. So did his friends: Vano, Annette, Koté, Braguine…"

He went quiet for a while. Then he smiled and said, "So you got to play my sister, Big Louis!"

Big Louis smiled, then shifted about a bit. He clearly had something he was dying to ask.

"What is it?" asked Kamo.

Big Louis took the plunge. "What I really want to know is how you managed to shake off that wolf who was following you. Don't tell me you've forgotten about him too?"

Kamo's smile revealed a row of shiny teeth. "Who knows?" he said gently. "Maybe I ate him, in the end."

A few days later, when Kamo's mother walked into her son's room, she said sharply, "So, as soon as I turn my back, you bang your head."

"What about you?" Kamo answered back. "As soon as I let you out of my sight, you play truant."

They were always like that with each other. They never let on how upset they were. They kept their worries to themselves, and they fought their fears on their own. They really loved each other.

"I wasn't going to find out anything about your great-grandfather on a tourist trip, now was I?"

Kamo's eyes lit up. "Well?" He was propped up on his elbows, watching his mother like a starving man. "Well? Did you find out how that Cossack-eater died?"

She nodded slowly, and stroked her son's bald head.

"Tell us."

She told us.

It was July 1922. The Russian Revolution had finished five years earlier. The civil war was also over. Mélissi the Greek – Mélissi the Bee – hadn't forgotten about her Kamo. He'd chosen the Revolution over her, yes; he'd fought the Cossacks, yes; but now he was free. She tried to track him down in the chaos of that vast country, and she succeeded. The new government had appointed Kamo chief customs officer in the Trans-Caucasus, and he was living in Tiflis. She took the train. He got a telegram: *It's me, I'm coming.*

The evening of her arrival, he jumped on a bike. He pedalled towards the station like a madman, shouting out her name in the night: "Mélissi!"

It was a black car. Travelling without lights. Very fast. On the wrong side of the road. Kamo wasn't exactly keeping to his side of the road either.

Kamo's mother interrupted her story for a moment. She opened her bag, took out something and held it out to her son.

"There you go – it's for you. The authorities gave it to me. It was the only thing in this world he cared about… It was a present from Mélissi."

Kamo took the present in the palm of his hand. It was an old-fashioned watch, with a sprung case and a gold chain. Kamo pressed a ridged button, and the watch cover opened. The glass was broken, and the hands had stopped moving.

They pointed to eleven.